W9-BJK-592

This book belongs to:

A catalogue record for this book is available from the British Library

Published by Ladybird Books Ltd
A subsidiary of the Penguin Group
A Pearson Company

LADYBIRD and the device of a Ladybird are trademarks of
Ladybird Books Ltd Loughborough Leicestershire UK
First published by Ladybird Books Ltd MCMXCVI. This edition MCMXCVII

This way Little Badger

by Phil McMylor
illustrated by Cliff Wright

The day was ending in the big wood.

Someone moved through the trees,
going very slowly...
searching high and low...
Little Badger and his sister, Belle.

Sister Belle knew the big wood well.
But everything was new
to Little Badger,
who had never in his life
been there before.

"Dig, Little Badger,"
said Sister Belle.
"A badger's claws
are made for digging!"

Sister Belle had big,
strong claws, but
Little Badger's claws
were small and soft.

The sun went down behind the trees.

“Keep close,” said Sister Belle.
“The dark is coming.”

But, when Sister Belle stopped
to eat a fat white grub,
Little Badger went off on his own
and was soon lost.

Owl swooped down from
the great oak tree and hooted,
"Hurry home, Little Badger!"

"But which way is home?"
cried Little Badger.
"Oh, I wish Sister Belle was
here to show me the way!"

"This way, Little Badger!"
called a voice in the bushes.

Little Badger snuffled deeper
into the wood.

"You're not Sister Belle!"
said Little Badger when he saw…

Rabbit.

“Watch out, the dark is coming!”
said Rabbit.

“Can I see it?”
asked Little Badger.

“No, but it can see you!
It has lots of eyes,”
answered Rabbit.
And he hopped into his burrow.

“This way, Little Badger!”
called a voice in the branches.

Little Badger snuffled deeper
into the wood.

“You’re not Sister Belle,”
said Little Badger when he saw…

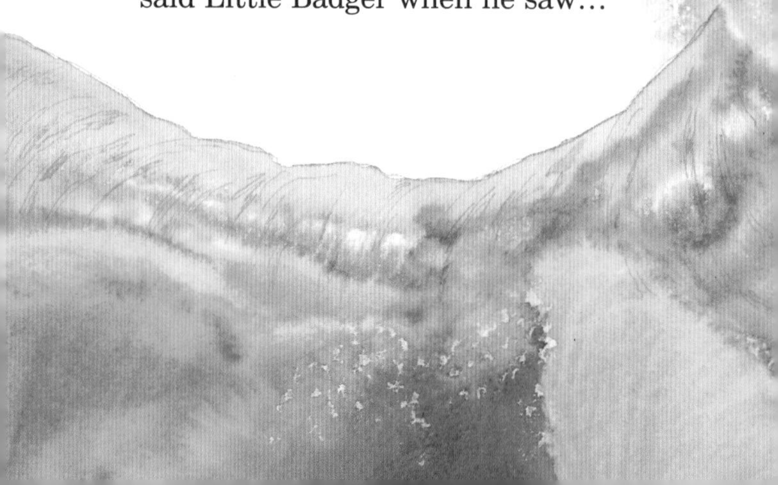

Magpie.

"Watch out, the dark is coming!"
said Magpie.

"Can I talk to it?"
asked Little Badger.

"No, but it can talk to you!
It has lots of voices,"
answered Magpie.
And she flew into her nest.

"This way, Little Badger!"
called a voice in the wet leaves.

Little Badger snuffled deeper
into the wood.

"You're not Sister Belle!"
said Little Badger when he saw...

Mouse.

“Watch out, the dark is coming!”
said Mouse.

“Can I touch it?”
asked Little Badger.

“No, but it can touch you!
It has lots of fingers,”
answered Mouse.
And he ran into his hole.

"What does the dark do when it
comes into the wood?"
asked Little Badger.

"It chases the daylight away,"
called Mouse from his hole.

"It fills in the spaces between the
branches and the leaves,"
called Magpie from her nest.

"It makes it hard to see,"
called Rabbit from his burrow.

"Owl can see!"
squeaked Mouse, trembling.

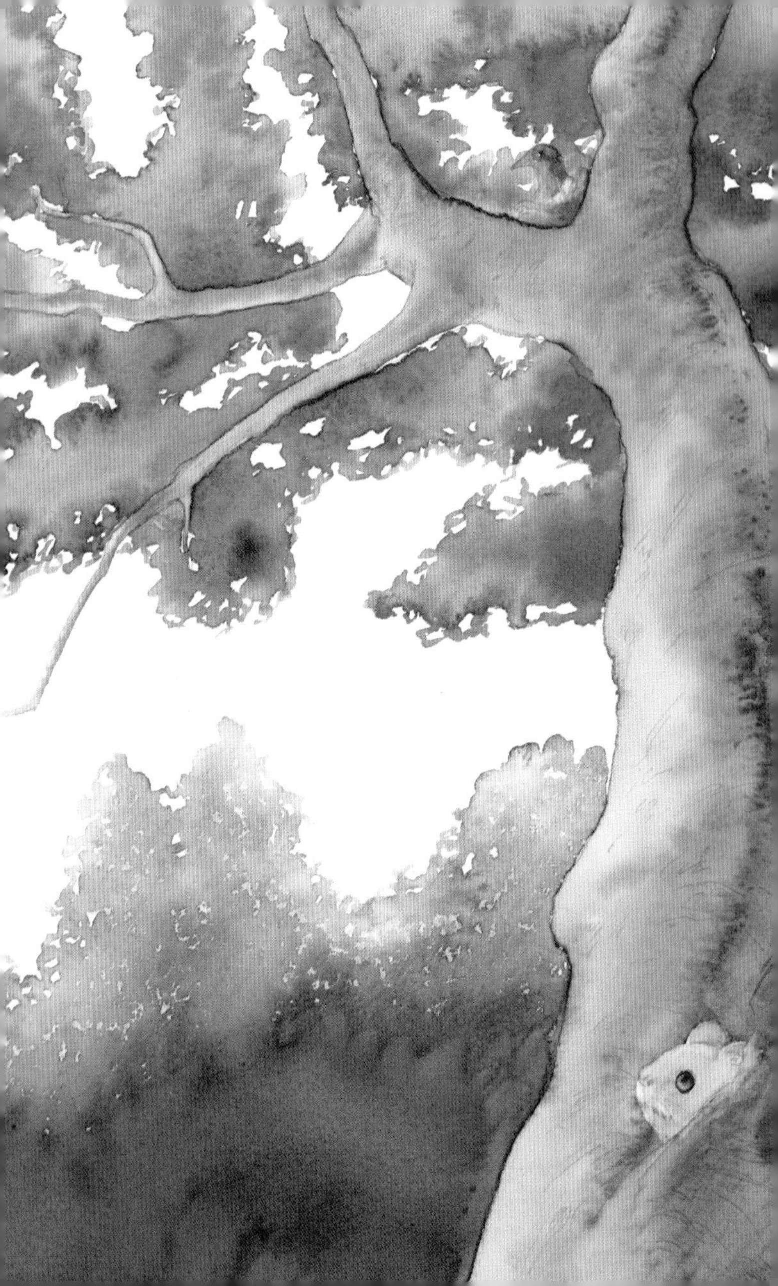

A voice from the edge
of the wood called,
"This way, Little Badger!"

"Is that you, Dark?"
called Little Badger.
But, only an echo answered...

DARK... DARK... DARK!

Owl flew off.
The other animals hid.
And Little Badger...

ran away.

He saw lots of eyes...
and he heard lots of voices.
He felt lots of fingers...
tugging at his fur.

He hid in a deep, inky hole.

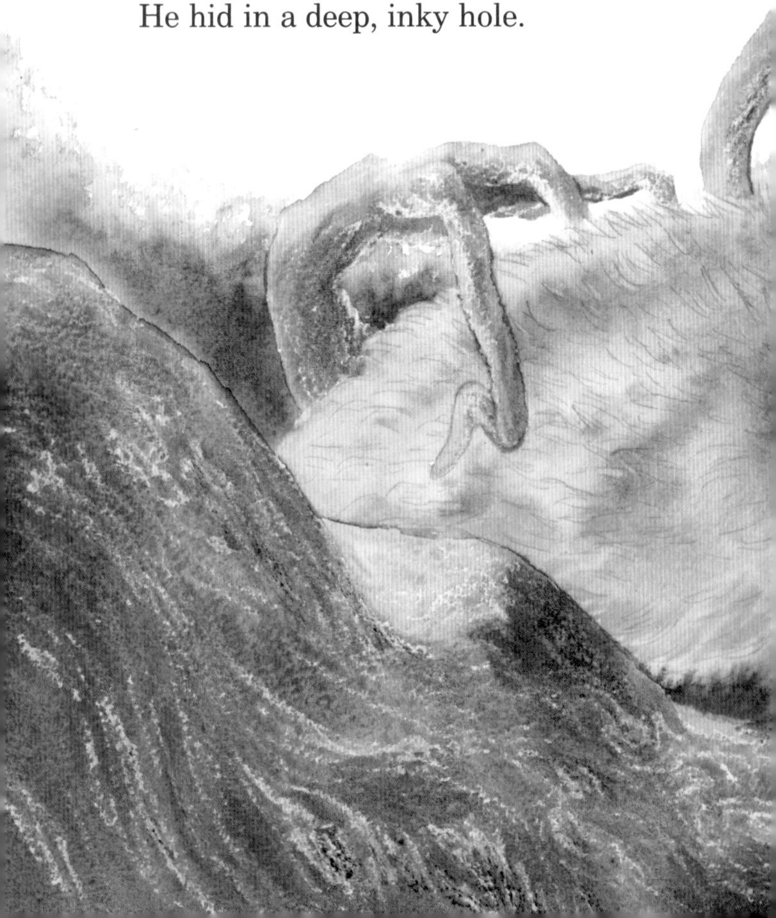

Little Badger whispered,
"Are you there, Dark?"

But only an echo answered…

DARK… DARK… DARK!

He tried to scramble out.
But the walls fell in.
Tree roots and damp earth
covered him from snout to tail.

"Dark has caught me!"
cried Little Badger.

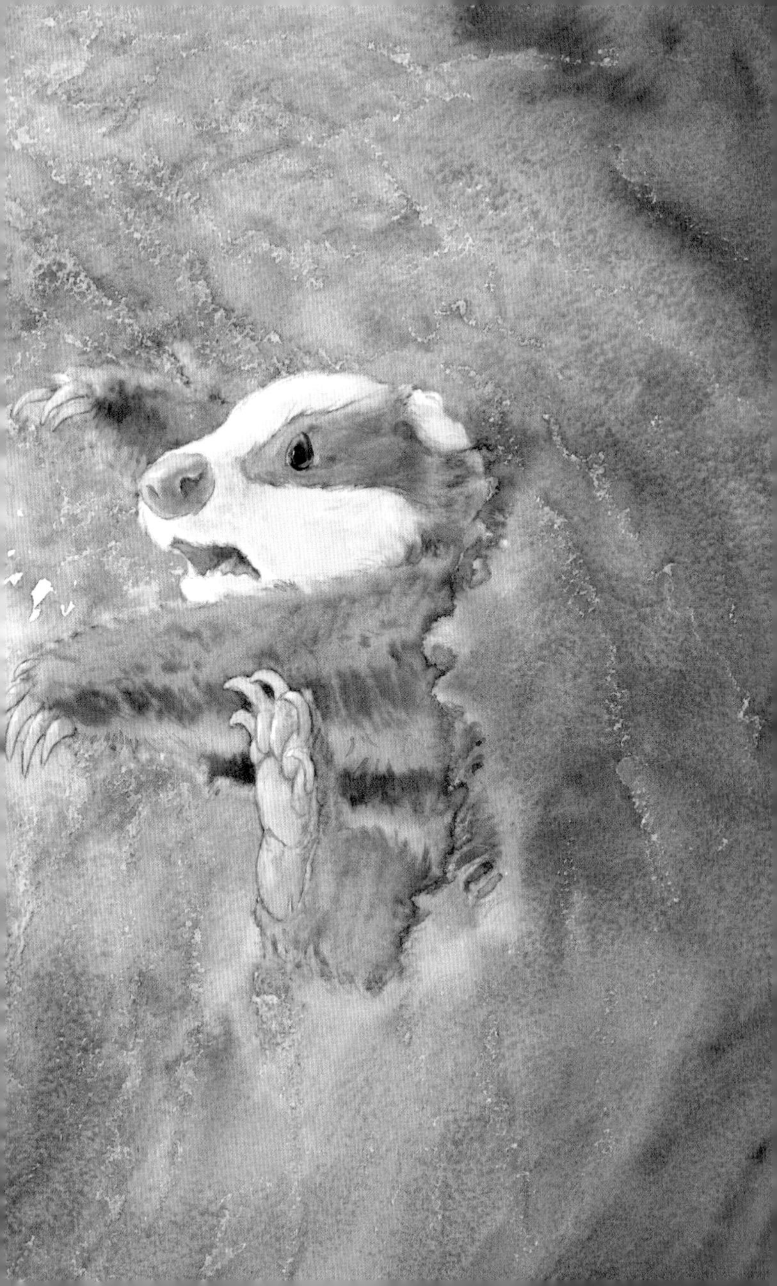

As he lay with the dark all about him,
Little Badger remembered what
Sister Belle had said:
A badger's claws are made for digging!

And Little Badger started to dig…

DIG… DIG… DIG!

And he didn't stop digging until he
was out of that deep, inky hole.

Little Badger shook the dirt out of his eyes.

Someone moved through the trees, going very slowly…
searching high and low.
Little Badger saw the moonlight glow.

"Hurrah!" he cried. "It's Sister Belle!"

"Oh, *there* you are, Little Badger," cried Sister Belle. "Where have you been?"

"I couldn't find you, Sister Belle. Then I got frightened and Dark was coming," whispered Little Badger.

"You had no need to be afraid," smiled Sister Belle. "A badger learns to like the dark."

"Yes," said Little Badger. "I like it now. I'll never be afraid again."

The moon came up behind the trees. The dark went out of the big wood.

Then Sister Belle said, "This way, Little Badger!"

And she took him home.